AUTUMN
PUBLISHING

Published in 2020
by Autumn Publishing
Cottage Farm
Sywell
NN6 0BJ
www.igloobooks.com

Autumn is an imprint of Bonnier Books UK

Based on the book: *'The Hundred and One Dalmatians'* by Dodie Smith
Published by the Viking Press.
'The Aristocats' based on the book by Thomas Rowe

0820 001
2 4 6 8 10 9 7 5 3 1
ISBN 978-1-83903-041-3

Printed and manufactured in China

This book belongs to

....

....

Contents

THE
LION KING
A Prince's Day

It was early morning at Pride Rock. Simba and Nala couldn't wait to go out and play. "Let's go down to the river!" Nala said loudly.

"Shhh," Simba whispered. "We have to be quiet or Zazu will hear us."

But it was too late. Zazu had been on the lookout for the young prince.

"Ahh! There you are, Simba," Zazu said, landing in front of Simba. "Come along. We have a busy day of training ahead of us."

"But Nala and I were about to go down to the river!" Simba complained.

"Nonsense," Zazu said. "As a prince you have certain responsibilities, young sire. And we can't keep them waiting."

"Bye, Simba!" Nala said. "Have fun at prince school! Maybe we can go to the river tomorrow."

"Not if Zazu has anything to say about it," Simba grumbled, watching as Nala bounded away.

Zazu led Simba down to the watering hole, where the animals of the Pride Lands were taking turns drinking water.

"Part of a ruler's responsibilities is solving disputes between his subjects. A perfect example is the watering hole! Each animal needs to have a turn to drink," Zazu explained. "See that herd of antelopes? They have been here too long. It's the rhinos' turn! You! You there!" the bird said, yelling at the antelopes.

Simba listened for what felt like hours as Zazu talked on and on to the antelopes.

Finally, the lion cub saw a chance to escape. A herd of giraffes was leaving the watering hole. If he could sneak out with them, he might still have time to play with Nala!

Just when Simba thought he had got away, Zazu landed in front of him.

"And where do you think you're going?" Zazu demanded.

"Come on, Zazu. We've been at the watering hole for hours. Can't I go play with Nala?" Simba asked.

But Zazu refused to let him go. "A prince's job is never done!" he insisted. "Onward to our next stop!"

Zazu led Simba back to Pride Rock, where Mufasa was listening to his subjects' concerns.

"A king must listen to all the other animals," Zazu explained. "You can learn a lot from your father."

Simba tried to pay attention. He listened as Mufasa advised the elephants to find new grazing grounds. He listened as the zebras worried about the upcoming rainy season.

But soon the lion cub was just as bored as he had been at the watering hole. He started to fall asleep.

"Young sire!" Zazu yelled, angrily pecking Simba awake. "Were you paying any attention at all?"

Simba yawned, shaking himself awake. He looked around. The other animals were gone. Mufasa must have finished for the day.

"Um, I heard some of it?" Simba replied.

Frustrated, Zazu flew up in the air. "Come along, Simba. We aren't finished yet," he said.

Simba slowly followed as the bird led him away from Pride Rock. Soon they were walking past the river where Simba and Nala had planned to play that day. Simba looked for his friend, but he didn't see her. Suddenly, Simba heard a yell.

"Did you hear that, Zazu?" he asked.

"Hear what, Simba?" Zazu said. There was another yell.

"That!" Simba said, running towards the river. Zazu flew after him.

It was Nala. She had fallen into the fast-moving river and couldn't get out!

"Hurry, go get my father!" Simba ordered Zazu.

The bird flew away in search of Mufasa, but Simba knew there wasn't time to wait. Nala needed him now!

Simba looked everywhere for a way to get to his best friend. Finally, he saw a long tree branch on the shore of the river.

"Nala! Grab on!" Simba yelled. He grabbed the branch in his mouth and moved it over the river. Nala reached out and grabbed it just in time!

Simba pulled the branch back and dragged Nala out of the river.

She was safe!

"Simba? Simba!" Mufasa called, running to the river.

"Here, Dad!" Simba said, panting. "It's okay! I got Nala!" Relieved, Mufasa and Zazu gathered the cubs and headed back to Pride Rock.

"Zazu, Nala, can you give me a moment with Simba?" Mufasa asked. Simba was worried. Was Mufasa angry at him for not paying attention to Zazu?

"Zazu told me about your day. I know that you want to play with your friend, but Zazu was trying to teach you important lessons about what it means to be king," Mufasa said.

"What did you learn at the watering hole?" Mufasa asked.

"That the rhinos follow the antelopes?" Simba replied. Mufasa laughed.

"No, that you have to be fair as a ruler and make sure all your subjects are treated equally," he said. "And Zazu brought you to Pride Rock to show you that a leader must be wise as well. But the last lesson you taught yourself."

"I did?" Simba said.

"Yes, my son. You rescued Nala and showed that a ruler must be brave. I am very proud of you, Simba."

Simba smiled up at his father.

"Now," Mufasa said, "I think there may just be enough time for you and Nala to play before dinner."

Simba smiled and bounded off to find Nala.

"He'll make a good king someday, sire," Zazu said, landing on Mufasa's shoulder.

Mufasa smiled. "Yes, he will."

Disney
Bambi
The Winter Trail

One winter morning, Bambi was sleeping softly when he heard a thumping sound nearby.

"Come on, Bambi!" his bunny friend, Thumper, called. "It's a perfect day for playing."

Bambi got up and followed Thumper through the forest. It was a beautiful day! The sky was blue and sunny, and the ground was covered in a blanket of new snow. Icicles glistened on the trees as Bambi and Thumper raced beneath the frozen branches.

As the two friends played, they came across a line of footprints in the snow.

"Look at these tracks!" Thumper said excitedly. "Who do you suppose they belong to?"

The friends decided to follow the footprints, hoping to meet the animal who had left the trail.

Before long, they came to a tree and saw someone who might have made the snowy tracks.

"Wake up, Friend Owl!" called Thumper. The bird peered down at the animals. He had flown to his favourite tree branch and only just fallen asleep.

"Stop that racket!" he replied crossly, and closed his eyes. Bambi and Thumper giggled. Friend Owl was always grouchy when they woke him up.

"Friend Owl, have you been out walking?" Bambi asked.

"Now why would I do that?" Friend Owl replied, opening his eyes. "My wings take me everywhere I need to go."

"Oh, I see," Thumper said. "Thanks anyway!"

So the two friends continued to follow the snowy footprints.

Soon, Bambi and Thumper met up with their friend Faline.

"You can help us find whoever made these tracks," said Bambi, pointing to the trail.

Faline nodded and began to walk with them.

"We should see if Flower wants to come, too," Faline said. Flower was their skunk friend.

But when they found Flower, he was fast asleep. Thumper tried to wake
Flower, but the little skunk just mumbled, "See you next spring," without even
opening his eyes.

The three friends decided to keep going without him.

Thumper bounded down the path. He followed the footprints to a frozen pond and glided across. "Come on!" he called. "There are tracks over here, too."

So Faline and Bambi started to cross the pond. Before long, Faline had joined Thumper on the other side. But Bambi wasn't a very good skater. His hooves slipped backwards and forwards until he fell flat on the ice!

"Aw, Bambi," Thumper giggled. "It's okay. We can go skating later, and I'll even show you how to spin around."

After a lot of slipping and sliding, Bambi finally took a running start and whizzed across the pond on his belly.

"You made it!" Faline cheered.

Next, the three friends walked up a snowy hill. At the top, they spotted a raccoon sitting by a tree trunk, eating some berries.

"Hello, Mr Raccoon," Faline said. "Did you happen to see who made these tracks in the snow?"

But the raccoon's mouth was so full he couldn't say anything! He shook his head and began tapping the tree.

The friends looked around. Then they heard a *tap-tap-tap* in the distance.
"I know!" Thumper cried. "He thinks we should ask the woodpeckers."
"Oh, thank you," Bambi said. The raccoon waved goodbye as the friends
headed down the path towards the woodpeckers' pine grove.

The tapping got louder and louder. Soon Bambi, Faline and
Thumper had found the woodpeckers. The mama was pecking away,
and her three children were sitting in holes in the tree trunk. They
stuck their heads out when they heard Thumper call, "Helloooooo!"

"Yes?" the mama bird replied.

"Did you make the tracks in the snow?" Thumper asked.

"No, we've been here all day," she answered.

"Yes, yes, yes," her babies added.

Just then, Faline noticed that the trail continued behind the tree.

Bambi and Thumper chatted excitedly as they walked. "If the tracks don't belong to the woodpeckers, and they don't belong to the raccoon, and they don't belong to Friend Owl, whose can they be?" Bambi asked.

Suddenly, Thumper stopped and looked down. They had finally reached the end of the trail! The tracks led all the way to a snowy bush, where a family of quail was resting.

"Did you make these tracks?" Thumper asked Mrs Quail.

"Why, yes," she answered. "Friend Owl told me about this wonderful bush. So this morning, my babies and I walked all the way over here."

Thumper, Bambi and Faline cheered. They had solved the mystery of the strange tracks – and they had spent a beautiful day visiting friends.

"Oh dear," Faline said as she saw the sun setting over the hill. "I think it's time for us to go home."

But when they turned to leave, a big surprise was waiting for them – their mothers!

Thumper was confused. "How did you find us?" he asked.

Thumper's mama answered, "Well, your sisters pointed us in the right direction and then..." She looked down at the deer and rabbit tracks that the three friends had left in the snow.

"You followed our trail!" Faline cried. Her mother nodded.

"Now, let's follow it back home," Bambi's mother said.

And that's just what they did.

Barking up the Right Tree

"**W**hat a day!" Tramp said, gazing out the window into the garden. "C'mon! What are we waitin' for? Let's go outside and do something fun!" he called to Lady.

Lady jumped up from her cosy cushion and happily padded towards the doggy door. "Why don't we play hide-and-seek?" she suggested.

"That's a great idea," said Tramp. "Last one outside is it!"

A few moments later, Tramp was busy counting.

"Seven... eight... nine... ten! Ready or not, here I come!" he said.

Tramp opened his eyes and quickly scanned the garden. He looked right.
He looked left. He looked up and down. Finally, he saw them: two dainty
pale-brown paws peeking out from beneath the flowers!

"Gotcha!" Tramp said, playfully pouncing paws-first into the flowers. "Me-ow!"

"Hey!" Tramp cried. The next thing he knew, a blur of soft brown and white fur was hurtling past him. Startled, he fell into a rosebush.

"What was that?" Lady gasped, jumping out from behind the doghouse, where she had been hiding.

Tramp pointed to the thick trunk of the shady old elm tree. A fluffy brown and white kitten was racing straight up to the nearest branch.

"Oh, poor thing," Lady cooed. "You must have scared her, Tramp."

"Scared her?" Tramp frowned, shaking the thorns out of his tail. "More like she scared me!"

"Oh, Tramp," said Lady teasingly. "Don't tell me a little kitten scared you. It's all right!" she called up to the kitten. "Tramp was only playing. We're sorry if you're frightened. Trust me, we'd never hurt you. It's perfectly safe to come back down."

The kitten peered down from her branch, looking scared.

"Oh, won't you please come down?" Lady urged her.

But the kitten didn't move.

"Awh! Lemme talk to her," said Tramp, stretching up to rest his front paws against the tree. "Here, kitty," he called. "C'mon down. I'm sorry. I know I can seem a little, uh, big and scary, but really, we were just playing a game of hide-and-seek."

At last, the kitten moved, but only to tiptoe farther along the branch.

"Looks like she's happy up there," Tramp said, shrugging.

"Or stuck!" Lady said. "Oh, Tramp, we have to help her down!"

Tramp didn't have much interest in helping the kitten out of the tree, but he would do anything for Lady. And Lady had a plan – a plan that seemed like it just might work if he helped her.

"You stand here, next to the tree and let me climb on your back," Lady told Tramp. "Then, maybe, if I stretch as far as I can, I can reach that kitten and help her down."

As it so happened, at that very moment, Jock was strolling by the garden and decided to drop in.

"Well, I must say! This is a grand sight!" he exclaimed as he spotted Tramp and Lady. "You certainly don't see somethin' like this every day, now do you? Would this be a new trick Darling and Jim Dear taught you?"

"Oh, no. It's no trick," Lady told Jock. She explained that she and Tramp were trying to help the kitten down from the tree.

"Unfortunately, I can't get high enough," Lady said.

"Aye, I can see that, lass," Jock replied.

"Maybe if you climbed up and stood on me..." Lady began.

"Say no more!" Jock gallantly told her. "As ever, my lady, I am at your service!"

A few minutes later, Trusty wandered over from his front porch.

"Well, I do declare," he said, even more surprised than Jock had been. "Miss Lady, what in the world are you and Jock doing up there?"

Lady explained the situation.

"I see, I see," Trusty said.

"Unfortunately," sighed Lady, "we still can't reach the kitten. But maybe if you helped us, Trusty?"

"Why, Miss Lady," replied Trusty, "what kind of gentleman would I be if I didn't oblige such a request?"

"Was that a yes or a no?" Tramp asked. "I can't tell."

"I believe that would be an aye," said Jock.

"Alrighty, then. Let's do this thing!" Tramp said.

Carefully, everyone climbed down. Then Tramp climbed onto Trusty's back, and Lady and Jock climbed back into place.

"Can you reach the branch now, Jock?" Lady called up to him.

"Aye!" said Jock, wagging his tail.

"Awoo!" howled Trusty, so happy that he didn't notice the butterfly landing on his nose... until it was too late.

Suddenly, Trusty's howl turned into a howling sneeze! Before the dogs knew it, their carefully constructed tower had collapsed into a furry twelve-legged pile. *Twelve legs?* Lady counted again. *Shouldn't there be sixteen legs?* she thought.

"Where's Jock?" she asked.

"Up here, lassie!"

Lady looked up, along with Tramp and Trusty, to see Jock dangling by his front paws from the branch.

"I don't suppose you could get back up here in a hurry," Jock called down as calmly as he could. "I'm having a wee bit of trouble holding on."

Quickly, the dogs re-formed their tower. At the bottom, Trusty kept an eye out for any butterflies, determined to hold his ground this time. At the top, Jock regained his footing on Lady's shoulders.

"Here, kitty, kitty..." he said gently. "Here—"

"Is something wrong?" Lady asked when Jock suddenly stopped.

"Aye," Jock answered, looking up and down the branch. "There is one wee problem, I'm afraid."

The kitten was not on the branch any more. In fact, the kitten wasn't even in the tree!

"Why, I do declare!" Trusty exclaimed, looking down. "If that li'l ol' kitten ain't a-rubbin' my back leg!"

"Aye, so she is!" Jock said.

"You've got to be kidding me," Tramp groaned.

"I just love happy endings, don't you?" Lady asked when everyone was back on the ground.

Jock and Trusty agreed.

"Yeah, they're okay, I guess," Tramp said as the kitten took a turn around his leg. "But you know what I like even better?"

"What?" Lady asked.

"Playing hide-and seek! Hey, kitten! You're it!"

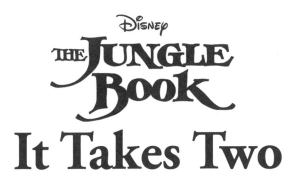

The Jungle Book
It Takes Two

"We did it!" Mowgli hollered. He had just escaped from King Louie and the apes with his friends Baloo and Bagheera.

"It sure was a swinging good time," Baloo said.

Bagheera was less enthusiastic.

"Next time, we need to stick to the plan! We're lucky to be alive."

"We need to find a safe place for the night," Bagheera said. "King Louie may still be after Mowgli."

"Aw, loosen up! I can protect us. If we see any of those mangy monkeys, I'll jab with my left, and I'll swing with my right—"

"Oh, Baloo. We need to protect the boy. Think about it," Bagheera said.

Mowgli sighed. He didn't need protecting. Why, with his strength, he could fight like a bear. And with his brains, he could plan like a panther... if only they'd give him the chance!

Just then Mowgli heard something. There was a rustling sound above his head, in the trees.

Mowgli giggled as a flying squirrel glided above him and landed on a branch. "I want to try that!" he shouted.

Mowgli climbed a tree and grabbed a vine. But try as he might, he just kept crashing to the ground.

Finally, Mowgli got the hang of it. He felt like he was flying!
He and the squirrel swept over the heads of Bagheera and Baloo.
Mowgli was having the time of his life, but soon his stomach
started grumbling.

"There are some bananas!" he told the squirrel, pointing across
a river. "Let's race!"

There was just one problem. Mowgli and his new friend didn't know how to cross the river. Mowgli looked at the vine he was holding and got an idea. "Let's swing," Mowgli said. "On the count of three: one, two, three...!"

Mowgli swung across the water. But his hands slipped, and he fell into the river.

Kaa, the snake, had been watching Mowgli. This was his chance to get the Man-cub.

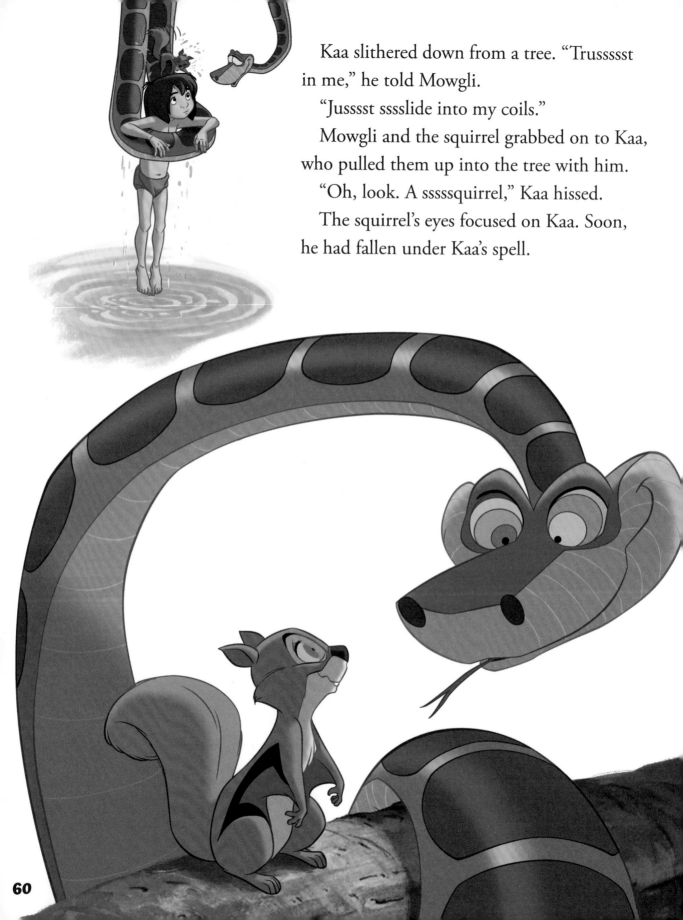

Kaa slithered down from a tree. "Trussssst in me," he told Mowgli.

"Jusssst sssslide into my coils."

Mowgli and the squirrel grabbed on to Kaa, who pulled them up into the tree with him.

"Oh, look. A sssssquirrel," Kaa hissed.

The squirrel's eyes focused on Kaa. Soon, he had fallen under Kaa's spell.

Using his brain, Mowgli realised that if he didn't look into Kaa's eyes, the snake could not make him go to sleep. And using his strength, Mowgli wrapped Kaa's tail around a stone and dropped it.

The snake fell from the tree.

"Ssssome thankssss I get!" Kaa muttered.

"Mowgli!"

"Little Britches!"

Bagheera and Baloo stood across the river, shouting.
They had been worried about Mowgli.

"I'm over here!" Mowgli hollered. "I used my brains and
my strength to save—"

"What? We can't hear you!" said Baloo.

Mowgli turned to look at his new friend. "Thanks for teaching me how to glide! I hope we meet again," he said. "Maybe next time I'll try gliding without the vine."

The squirrel chittered at Mowgli and then flew away, high above the ground.

"Hmmm," Mowgli said, watching the squirrel take flight. "Maybe that's not such a good idea after all."

Mowgli made his way downriver, past the waterfalls.

On the other side of the river, Bagheera and Baloo followed him. When he reached a patch of calm water, Mowgli swung – and swam – to his friends.

Mowgli threw himself into Baloo's arms. He'd had a fun adventure, but he was glad to be back with his friends.

That night, as Mowgli drifted off to sleep, he heard his friends still arguing.

"He used brains. He didn't look into Kaa's eyes," Bagheera said.

"It was strength! He used a big rock to get rid of Kaa," Baloo argued.

Mowgli smiled. He had used his brains *and* his strength to save himself and his new friend today!

Pinocchio
A Real Boy

The sun was just beginning to rise over Pinocchio's little village. The moment he awoke, Pinocchio leapt out of bed and ran to look at himself in the mirror.

He laughed with joy when he saw his reflection. It hadn't been a dream. The Blue Fairy had made him a real boy!

Pinocchio lost track of the minutes as he stared at his reflection.

He might have stood there all day if he hadn't smelled a wonderful scent coming from the kitchen.

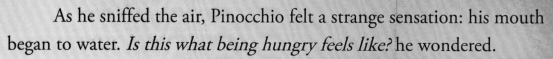

As he sniffed the air, Pinocchio felt a strange sensation: his mouth began to water. *Is this what being hungry feels like?* he wondered.

Pinocchio put on his clothes and ran to the kitchen. There he saw his father, Geppetto, cooking a huge breakfast. There were eggs and pancakes and bacon and sausages and oatmeal and orange juice and toast and milk and muffins and... Pinocchio stopped trying to name everything on the table.

Geppetto grinned when he saw Pinocchio. "I wanted to cook you something special for your first breakfast, but I couldn't decide what to make," he said. "So I made everything!"

Pinocchio's stomach rumbled as he looked at all the food.

"Well, come on," Geppetto said. "Dig in!"

Pinocchio sat down and tried a bite of eggs.

"It's fluffy!" he said, his mouth full. "And soft. And... delicious!"

Pinocchio tried a little bit of all the food Geppetto had made. Every bite tasted different from the last.

"This is wonderful," Pinocchio said. "Can we eat all day long?"

"Oh, no," Geppetto laughed. "We'll be much too busy for that. I have so much to show you."

"Can we take the food with us?" Pinocchio asked.

"That's an excellent idea," Geppetto said. "We'll have a picnic!"

Geppetto packed up a lunch, and he and Pinocchio left to explore the village.

The first thing Pinocchio noticed was how brightly the sun shone. He blinked as he left the dark cottage and walked into the sunshine. The dazzling beams felt warm against his skin. He quickly discovered that stepping into the long shadows of the buildings cooled him down again. Pinocchio and Geppetto made a game of running in and out of the shadows all the way to the edge of town. When Pinocchio jumped through the last shadow, he felt a strange sensation in his stomach. It was different from hunger. It was—

Hic! Pinocchio's tummy flip-flopped and a strange sound came from his throat.

"What—*hic*—is going—*hic*—on?" Pinocchio asked. He was starting
to get scared.

"Don't worry," Geppetto said. "It's just the hiccups."

"Hiccups?" Pinocchio asked. "Will they ever—*hic*—stop?"

Geppetto showed Pinocchio how to hold his breath until
the hiccups went away.

Pinocchio wasn't sure he liked this new experience. He had been so busy
thinking about how much fun being a real boy was, he hadn't stopped to think
about all the things that could go wrong.

Pinocchio grew silent as he followed Geppetto. His mind was filled with questions, but he wasn't sure how to ask many of them. At first, the sun's warmth had felt nice. But now Pinocchio was hot and sweaty. His feet hurt. And his stomach felt as empty as it had that morning before breakfast.

Pinocchio finally asked the question he was most concerned about: "Are we there yet?"

Geppetto took Pinocchio's hand. "It's just over this hill..."

The pair climbed higher until they saw a beautiful valley below them.

"Race you to the swimming hole?" Geppetto asked. Pinocchio nodded and ran off before Geppetto was even prepared! Father and son ran down the hill and collapsed in a happy pile next to the lake's edge.

"Time for food!" Pinocchio cheered.

Geppetto laughed and began unpacking the picnic basket.

Geppetto and Pinocchio spent the rest of the day at the swimming hole, playing in the water and fishing on the bank.

As they played, Geppetto told Pinocchio stories of the many times he had visited the lake as a young boy. Pinocchio felt much better now that he had eaten and rested. The cool water was refreshing after their long walk from the village. Even when Pinocchio scraped his knee on one of the willow trees, he didn't get upset. He was starting to realise what an exciting place the world was.

As the sun began to set, Pinocchio noticed a new feeling.
His eyelids felt heavy, as though he could barely keep his eyes open.
Then he yawned.

"I'm tired," Pinocchio said, surprised at the realisation.

"You've had quite a big day," Geppetto said.
"Are you ready to go home?"

Pinocchio nodded, and Geppetto lifted him onto his shoulders. He carried Pinocchio towards their little house in the village. Sitting on Geppetto's back, Pinocchio looked up into the night sky.

Far above them shone the Wishing Star, twinkling brightly. Pinocchio realised that being a real boy was more complicated than he had imagined.

"Today was fun, Father," Pinocchio said. "But... it was hard, too."

Geppetto nodded, thinking about what Pinocchio had said.

"That's what being alive is. It's sunlight and bacon and hiccups and scraped knees. Some of it will be scary, but I promise I'll be right there with you."

Geppetto waited for Pinocchio to answer, but all he heard was the sound of soft snoring. Pinocchio was fast asleep! Geppetto laughed quietly.

"Enough speeches. It's time to get you to bed."

Geppetto carried Pinocchio as gently as he could to bed.
He fluffed each pillow and then let his son snuggle down on the
soft sheets.

"Goodnight, my boy," Geppetto said, leaning in to kiss
Pinocchio on the forehead. "Today was a dream come true.
I cannot wait to share another adventure with you tomorrow."

DISNEY
THE ARISTOCATS
The Birthday Wish

"Good night, my loves," Duchess said. Her tail swished softly as she gave each of her kittens – Berlioz, Toulouse and Marie – a tender nuzzle.

"Sleep tight, kiddos," O'Malley said as he tucked them in. Berlioz and Toulouse purred happily, but Marie didn't want to go to bed.

"Please may I go to the party tonight?" she asked. "I promise to be very good!"

Duchess smiled and shook her head. "Scat Cat will have other birthday parties you can go to when you're older. For now, you need a good night's sleep."

Duchess and O'Malley left and shut the door quietly behind them. Marie listened as Berlioz began to snore softly. Then Toulouse's whiskers began twitching. Soon both of her brothers were fast asleep.

But Marie was wide awake.

Voices drifted from downstairs, then music. Duchess and O'Malley were throwing a birthday party for their friend Scat Cat. He was a jazz musician who had helped Duchess and the kittens when they were separated from their owner. Marie sighed. Oh, how she wished she were allowed to join them! Why, Scat Cat was her friend, too. It wasn't fair! After all, Marie could laugh and dance and sing as well as any grown-up.

That's it! Marie thought. She could sneak into the party if she looked like an adult. Tiptoeing carefully, she made her way down the stairs. The coat closet would be full of things she could use to disguise herself!

The noise from the ballroom became louder as Marie slipped into the dark closet. She rummaged around, trying things on. The feather boa tickled her nose. The frilly bonnet wasn't glamorous enough for a party. The dark glasses made it impossible for Marie to see anything. Finally, she found the perfect disguise. Marie thought she looked very grown-up.

Marie crept into the parlour and looked around. Scat Cat was leading the band in a fast-paced jazz number. Duchess and O'Malley were chatting with some cats in the corner. But most of the cats were dancing. They danced on the floor, on tables – there was even a cat swinging from the chandelier!

Marie wanted to dance, too. "But I have to stay quiet," she reminded herself. "I mustn't get caught!"

"This is a beautiful house," someone said. Marie turned around to see a lady cat wearing a sparkly collar. She was talking to Marie!

"Thank you," Marie said. Then she slapped a paw over her mouth.

She was in disguise as a guest. No one could know this was her house!

"I mean," Marie added in a hurry, "I think so, too."

The lady cat gave Marie a funny look. Marie decided to change the subject, fast.

"I like your collar," she said.

"I like your hat," the cat said. Marie beamed. It was working! Her disguise was perfect.

Nearby, a cat in an apron appeared, carrying a large platter.

"Who wants tuna ice cream?" he said.

"I do! I do!" Marie raised her paw and jumped up and down. Then she remembered – she was supposed to act like a grown-up tonight!

The aproned cat handed her a bowl.

"Thank you very much, young fellow," Marie said in her best adult voice. As she tasted the ice cream, she purred loudly. Tuna was her favourite!

Later, some of the guests played party games. Marie enjoyed the charades, but Pin the Tail on the Doggie was her favourite. She won every round!

As Marie removed her blindfold, the band started playing a new tune. Scat Cat put his trumpet down.

"You're on your own, fellas!" he said to the band. "This birthday cat has got a date with the dancefloor." Scat Cat walked over to Marie.

"Ma'am," he said with a wink, "may I have this dance?"

Marie forgot all about getting in trouble. She put her little paw in his, and Scat Cat led her out onto the dance floor.

"Enjoying the party, Marie?" Scat Cat asked.

"Oh, yes!" Marie replied. Then she gasped. "I mean... who's Marie?" she asked, trying to cover up her mistake.

"Don't worry. Your secret is safe with me," Scat Cat said. "Let's just dance!"

The music swelled, and Marie took Scat Cat's advice.
She swayed, bopped and jumped to the beat. Then, as the
piano trilled, Scat Cat spun her around like a top. Marie
whirled – and her disguise came flying off!

"Marie!"

The music stopped, and everyone stared. Marie's disguise was gone, and her mother was marching right towards her!

"Young lady, you are supposed to be in bed!" Duchess said. Marie looked up sadly. "I'm sorry, Mama," she said. "I didn't mean to disappoint you." Marie felt terrible for making her mother angry.

"Hey now," said a rumbly voice. Marie looked up. It was Scat Cat!
"Say, Duchess, it is my birthday," Scat Cat said, "and Marie's my friend.
How about letting her stay?" Scat Cat leaned over towards the birthday cake
on the table. "It's my birthday wish!" he said. Then he blew out all the candles
and winked at Marie. She smiled back.

Duchess sighed, looking closely at Marie and Scat Cat.

"Well, just this once, I suppose. But you are going to bed early tomorrow
night, Marie. Understood?"

Marie nodded happily. "Thank you, Mama! I promise I'll never sneak
out again."

So Marie stayed at the party, singing and dancing and talking with the grown-ups. Finally, it was time for everyone to go home.

Marie was as sleepy as she had ever been. As Duchess carried her up to bed, Marie heard Scat Cat call, "Thanks for coming to my party, Marie!"

"Happy birthday, Scat Cat!" Marie called back. "Thank you for the dance!"

Marie couldn't stop smiling as Duchess tucked her back into bed with her brothers. She would never forget her special night and Scat Cat's birthday wish!

Disney
Robin hood
Castle Rescue

Robin Hood whistled as he stirred a pot of soup. The hero was hidden deep in Sherwood Forest. His job had become very hard lately. Prince John and the Sheriff were trying their best to capture him.

Luckily, Robin Hood had good friends on his side. Little John, Friar Tuck and Maid Marian were all helping him come up with plans to help the people of Nottingham.

"Don't burn the soup, Rob!" Little John called as he and Maid Marian arrived with wood for the fire.

"I'll only make that mistake once," Robin Hood answered, handing out soup to his friends. Robin was about to take a sip when Friar Tuck appeared! The friar was out of breath and looked very worried.

"Friar Tuck! Is something wrong?" Maid Marian asked.

"Skippy is missing!" Friar Tuck said. He explained that Skippy, the young rabbit, had lost an arrow in Prince John's castle and gone in looking for it. His friend Toby had waited a long time for him to come back, but Skippy had never returned.

"He must be lost in the castle," Maid Marian said.

"Or worse, Prince John has caught him," Robin said. "I have to rescue Skippy." The fox grabbed his bow and arrows and headed towards the castle.

"I'm coming with you," Maid Marian said.

Robin Hood tried to tell her that it was too dangerous, but Marian wouldn't take no for an answer.

"I lived in the castle for years," she said. "I know it better than anyone. I'm your best chance to find Skippy before Prince John does. Plus, I know a secret passageway into the castle."

With Little John in tow, Robin Hood and Maid Marian soon made it inside the castle. They snuck up and down winding hallways, searching for Skippy at every turn.

Just as they were about to turn another corner, Robin Hood pulled Maid Marian back. He could hear voices coming right for them!

"Quick! We have to turn around!" Robin Hood said. But it was too late. There were voices coming from behind them, too. They were trapped!

Luckily, Robin had an idea. He tied a rope to a notch in the window.
Then he tied the other end to an arrow and fired it into another window on the
castle's opposite wall.

Robin gave the rope a good yank and then motioned for Maid Marian and
Little John to follow him. Cautiously, they shuffled behind him.

"Hurry!" Robin Hood said, leading the way across the rope.
He peeked into the window across from them. Everything looked quiet.
"Quick, through here!" Robin Hood said, pointing to a nearby door.

"This room looks familiar," Maid Marian said. But Maid Marian's realisation was too late. Robin Hood had already gone through the door –right into Sir Hiss's study. Even worse, Sir Hiss was there!

Maid Marian pointed to a door on the other side of the room. Very slowly, the group crept behind Sir Hiss. Luckily, Sir Hiss was in the middle of doing something very, very important: examining himself in the mirror.

"Sir Hiss, you've outdone yourself with this one!" the snake said to himself as he tried on a new hat. Robin opened the door and motioned his friends through.

They were safe!

Sir Hiss's room opened up into a large courtyard.

"There!" Little John whispered, pointing to one end of the courtyard. It was Skippy! The rabbit was hiding behind the well.

"Oh, no!" Maid Marian said, pointing at the opposite end of the courtyard. It was Prince John. He was walking right to Skippy's hiding place!

Robin looked everywhere for an escape route, but they were running out of time. The heroes had to keep Prince John from seeing Skippy.

"Quick, get Skippy out of the castle! I'll meet you back at the forest," Robin told his friends. Before they could argue with him, the fox climbed onto the castle's roof and yelled down at Prince John!

"Looking for me?" he called.

"You! Guards, seize him! Seize him!" Prince John ordered.

Guards rushed outside and began to shoot arrows at Robin! He ducked behind a chimney, avoiding the arrows just in time. Prince John was so distracted, he didn't notice Little John and Maid Marian in the courtyard. The pair grabbed Skippy and rushed him to the secret passageway.

Seeing that his friends were safe, Robin Hood leapt across the roofs away from Prince John.

"Always a pleasure!" he called back over his shoulder.

Back in the forest, Skippy, Maid Marian and Little John waited for Robin.

"I hope he's okay," Skippy said.

"Of course I am!" Robin said, appearing out of the trees.

"Robin!" Maid Marian said. "We were worried!"

"I'm safe and sound," Robin said. "And I found something in the castle. Try not to lose this again, Skippy!" He handed Skippy his missing arrow.

"Now, who would like some soup?"

Disney
Peter Pan
Captain Hook's Shadow

"Walk the plank, Peter Pan!" John Darling yelled, waving a wooden sword at his brother, Michael. The boys were playing in their nursery. John was pretending to be Captain Hook, and Michael was pretending to be Peter Pan.

"All right, John and Michael, time for bed," Wendy said, walking into the room.

"Just five more minutes?" John pleaded.

"You'll have plenty of time to walk the plank tomorrow," Wendy said.

Michael and John put down their swords and dutifully crawled into their beds.

Soon John and Wendy were fast asleep. Michael squeezed his eyes shut, but it was no use. He kept picturing Captain Hook trying to capture Peter Pan.

Suddenly, Michael heard a rattling sound, followed by a loud whoosh!

He opened his eyes and looked around. The nursery windows were thrown wide open, but no one was there!

Then Michael noticed a shadow against the far wall. He gasped in fear. The shadow looked just like Captain Hook!

Michael wanted to run, but he couldn't. He would have to hide.

Michael quickly dived under the covers. Captain Hook was scary! But being under the covers didn't make Michael feel any better. He needed to know if the pirate was in the nursery. Slowly, he lifted the bottom edge of his blanket and peeked out.

Michael still couldn't see Hook, but the captain's shadow was right there against the wall – as large as life. The shadow looked around the nursery for a moment. Then it began to creep towards the far corner.

A chill ran down Michael's spine.

Captain Hook was heading right towards Wendy!

Michael knew he had to protect his sister. As he glanced around the nursery, his eyes fell on his wooden sword.

Michael reached down and grabbed the sword just as the shadow got to Wendy. He threw off his covers and leapt towards it!

The shadow stumbled backward. Michael lunged at it again, but it swiped at him with its hook!

Michael dived under his bed. The shadow reached for him, but he darted away just in time!

The shadow jumped onto the bed. Michael gulped, waiting for the hook to swipe at him again. He wondered why he was seeing only Captain Hook's shadow. Where was Hook hiding?

Michael knew he had to do something. He couldn't stay under the bed forever. Captain Hook was sure to get him sooner or later!

Summoning all his courage, Michael dashed into the middle of the room, but the shadow came after him. As he tried to get away, he tripped over a ball.

The shadow skulked towards him. Shivering, Michael pictured the Crocodile that waited for anyone who walked the plank.

Suddenly, Michael heard someone call out, "Cock-a-doodle-doo!"

"Peter Pan!" Michael shouted as his hero flew in. "I'm so glad you're here! Captain Hook tried to get Wendy, but I stopped him."

"Hook is here?" Peter asked, looking around. "Why, it's Captain Hook's shadow. Don't let it get away!"

The shadow tried to run, but Peter flew after it.

"It's only a shadow?" Michael asked.
Suddenly, he wasn't so scared.

He leapt up from the floor and ran after it,
too.

"Grab it from the other side!" Peter called.
Michael ran towards the shadow from the
right as Peter flew at it from the left.

The shadow was trapped! In a flash,
Michael reached out and caught it.

"Put it in here!" Peter cried, holding out a sack.

Michael stuffed the shadow into the sack, and Peter tied it closed.

"That was close," Peter said.

"Why was Captain Hook's shadow here?" Michael asked.

"I stole the shadow for a prank," Peter explained. "Some prank! The shadow has been nothing but trouble. It pulled the Lost Boys' tails and put pinecones in their beds. And then it flew away from Never Land to cause trouble in London."

"That sounds really awful!" Michael cried, looking at Peter with wide eyes. "I'm glad we caught it!"

Peter nodded.

"Thanks for all of your help, Michael! I'd better fly back to Never Land and return it right away, while everyone aboard Captain Hook's ship is still asleep. Those nasty pirates have already caused enough trouble!"

"Do you want to come with me?" Peter asked Michael.
"It'll be a great adventure!"

"Not without Wendy and John," Michael replied.

"Then let's take them!" Peter said, flying over to Wendy's bed.
He reached down to give her a gentle shake, then drew his hand back.

"Aw, she's fast asleep." He looked over at John and said,
"John's asleep, too."

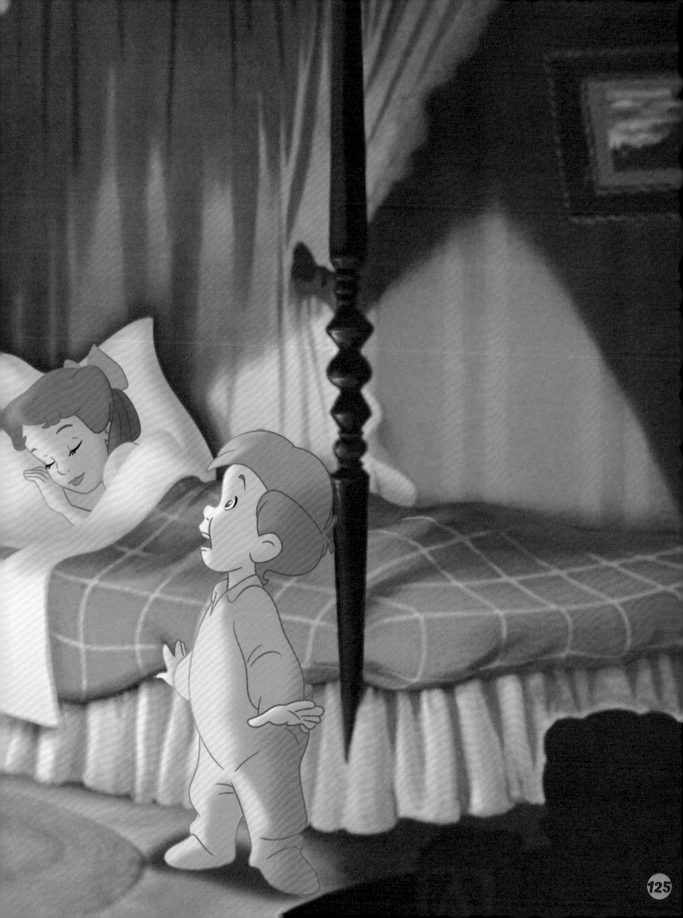

"Maybe next time," Peter said,
jumping to the window ledge.
"Goodbye, Michael. Tell Wendy
and John that I said hello!" he called.
Then he flew out into the night.
"I will!" Michael promised.
He waved goodnight and then went back
to bed, smiling. He was glad to have had
another adventure with Peter.

Disney
Lilo & Stitch
The Dog Show

In the middle of the Pacific Ocean, on the little island of Kauai, there lived a girl named Lilo and her pet, Stitch. Lilo was no ordinary girl. She loved doing everything her own way. And Stitch was no ordinary pet. He was an alien from outer space!

Every weekend, Lilo went to a dance class with the other girls from her town, while Stitch waited patiently outside. But today was different. Today there was another pet waiting outside with Stitch.

When dance class was over, Lilo's classmate Myrtle introduced Lilo and Stitch to her new dog.

"Her name is Cashmere. She's a purebred poodle." Myrtle scowled down at Stitch, who was eating a scoop of ice cream off the pavement. "Breeding is so important when it comes to pets," she said.

Lilo was embarrassed. She tried to ignore the mean things Myrtle said to her and Stitch, but it wasn't easy.

"Stitch might not be like other dogs, but he's really smart!" Lilo said. Just then, Stitch started rolling around in the melted ice cream.

"If Stitch is so smart," Myrtle said, "prove it." She handed Lilo a flyer. "There's a dog show next weekend. Cashmere and I are planning to win, and we'd love to beat you and Stitch."

Myrtle waved as she and Cashmere strutted away. Lilo and Stitch both growled, and Lilo crumbled the flyer into a tight ball. Stitch nuzzled against Lilo. He glanced around to see if anyone could hear him.

"Bully," he said.

But Lilo was already smoothing out the dog show flyer.

"I'm tired of Myrtle being mean to us. Let's show her and Cashmere what we can do, Stitch!"

Stitch looked at Lilo and then nodded. "For Lilo."

The next weekend, Lilo and Stitch showed up at the dog show. They were ready. At least, they hoped they were. But as the judges led everyone onto the stage, Lilo started to get nervous. She was glad her sister, Nani, had come along to cheer them on.

"Welcome, everyone," a friendly man with a microphone announced. "Let's start the show with a classic."

The man gestured to a row of hoops.

"Whichever dog can clear these hoops the fastest will win this round. Up first: Lilo and her dog, Stitch!"

Lilo sized up the rings. It would be a tight fit, but she was sure Stitch could zoom though them.

"Go, Stitch. Go!" Lilo shouted.

Stitch took a deep breath and then ran towards the rings. He grabbed the first ring... and immediately shoved it in his mouth. He managed to swallow it whole and then chomped down the next four rings. He ran happily back to Lilo and whispered, "Clear!"

"No, Stitch," Lilo sighed. "You were supposed to jump through the rings."

Stitch's ears drooped. "Sorry." He burped and then looked back at the shocked audience.

"Well, that's one way to clear rings," the man with the microphone said. "It's a good thing we have some extra rings for our next contestants!"

Soon the extra rings were set up. Cashmere sped through them and happily bounded back to Myrtle.

"It's okay, Stitch," Lilo said. "We have two events left. We can still win!" Stitch nodded eagerly.

"On to the next challenge," the man with the microphone shouted as the judges placed three tubes in a zigzag shape on the ground. "In order to complete this event, each dog must run through the three tubes to get to the other side of the course!"

Lilo and Stitch were up first again. "I know you can do this, Stitch," Lilo said. "Just try not to eat anything."

Stitch licked Lilo playfully and got into position.

"Ready. Set. Go!" the man with the microphone yelled. Like a bullet, Stitch shot out from the starting line and ran towards the first tunnel. But instead of running inside the tubes, the powerful alien smashed through the sides of each of them, running in a straight line from one side of the course to the other.

Stitch crossed the finish line and looked back at the judges proudly. Then he saw Lilo holding her head. Stitch hung his head. He knew he must have done something wrong.

"It's okay. Come here, boy," Lilo called to Stitch.

When Stitch reached her, Lilo said, "I don't think they're going to give us any points for that one, but we still have one event left."

Stitch watched sadly as Cashmere easily navigated the extra tubes. She and Myrtle had so many points, there was no way that Lilo and Stitch could win now.

The last challenge was to cross a balance beam.

"They don't have an extra balance beam, so you'll have to go last," Myrtle told Lilo.

Lilo wanted to say something mean back to Myrtle, but she took a deep breath instead.

"Good luck, Cashmere," she said through gritted teeth.

Lilo watched as Cashmere crossed the balance beam. She was perfect. One of the judges even said she'd never seen a dog with more poise.

Lilo and Stitch waited for every other dog to cross the beam. Finally, it was Stitch's turn.

"Okay, Stitch. Run as fast as you can!" Lilo said. Stitch nodded and raced towards the beam. One quick hop and he was already halfway across the thin platform. He turned back to smile at Lilo.

But as he did, he tripped on the beam. Stitch scratched at the side of the beam frantically. Most dogs would have fallen off the side, but Stitch was no dog. He used his alien arms to keep crawling along the bottom of the beam instead!

The crowd gasped as Stitch dismounted on the other side.

"I think we'd better go," Lilo said quickly.

Lilo ran to Nani and asked her to take them home.

"Don't you want to stay for the results?" Nani asked. Lilo shook her head. "No. I think we all know who's going to win."

She watched as one of the judges rushed to shake Myrtle's hand. Stitch whimpered beside Lilo. He felt bad for not doing better at the show.

"It's okay, Stitch," Lilo said. "It was my fault. I should have given better instructions."

Nani watched as Lilo hugged Stitch.

That night, Nani tucked Lilo and Stitch into bed.

"Don't laugh, but I made you something," she said, pulling out two large, flat rocks wrapped in shiny tin foil. "They're supposed to be medals," she mumbled, blushing.

Lilo and Stitch turned the rocks over. On the backs, Nani had written their names and the words 'Most Creative'.

"You did finish all the challenges. You just did them in your own way."

"Thank you, Nani," Lilo said, giving her sister a hug.

"Yes, thanks for Nani," Stitch said, joining the hug. He may not have won the dog show, but he had something even better... a family that loved him no matter what!

Disney 101 DALMATIANS
Detective Lucky

A blustery wind was blowing outside, but the Dalmatian puppies – all ninety-nine of them – were snug and cosy in their new house. The puppies crowded around Nanny, who was reading them a bedtime story.

Lucky loved bedtime stories. He especially loved ones about detectives! He wished he could be a detective, too.

When Nanny's story was over, Pongo and Perdita tucked the puppies into bed. But Lucky wasn't tired – not even a little bit! He couldn't stop thinking about all the mysteries he would solve if he were a detective.

One by one, the other puppies drifted off to sleep. Soon Lucky was the only one still awake. Suddenly, his ears twitched.

Creak, squeak, BANG!

What was that strange sound? Lucky bolted upright. Maybe this was it – the mystery he had wished for. Maybe the sound was a clue!

Lucky carefully climbed out of bed. His parents were in the living room with
Roger and Anita. No one would notice if Lucky slipped through the doggy door.
He could go outside, find some clues, crack the case and be back before anyone
even knew that he'd left!

Lucky scampered outside. He looked around. He had never been outside alone at night. The wind had died down, but it was very dark. All around him, Lucky saw strange shadowy shapes.

Lucky thought about going back inside. But he knew that a true detective would solve his case no matter what. If he wanted to be a detective, he'd have to go on, dark or no dark.

Lucky sniffed the air. An unfamiliar smell made his nose twitch. Maybe it was another clue!

Lucky pressed his nose down to the dirt and sniffed again. There it was – the same smell! His tail wagged as he followed the scent into the woods.

This is exactly what a real detective would do! Lucky thought eagerly as he tracked the smell to a hollow log. Lucky poked his head into the log to see what was inside – and found two spooky eyes staring back at him!

Lucky yelped in surprise. He backed out of the log as quickly as he could – and ran right into a tree.

Thunk!

Strange noises filled the air, and Lucky felt something brush by his head.

Hoo-hoo-hoo-hoo!

Flap-flap-flap-whooooooosh!

Lucky was surrounded by spooky sounds, and he didn't know what was making any of them. And to make matters worse, he'd been so busy tracking the smell that he hadn't noticed how far he'd roamed. He had no idea where he was or how to get home!

There was only one thing to do. Run!

Lucky raced through the forest, ducking under branches and leaping over rocks. When the trees began to thin, he charged forward, running faster and faster until – *wham!* He knocked right into someone!

In a flurry of fur and tails and hisses and growls, Lucky and the stranger tumbled over and over and over. Then a familiar voice said, "Lucky? Is that you?"

It was Sergeant Tibs, the cat who'd helped rescue Lucky and his siblings from Cruella De Vil!

"Sergeant Tibs!" Lucky cried in relief. "Help! I'm lost and I don't know how to get home!"

Sergeant Tibs knew just what to do. He led Lucky to an old barn, where the two filled the Colonel in on Lucky's situation.

"No question about it, we've got to get this pup back to the Dalmatian Plantation," the Colonel announced. "But it's too late for the Twilight Bark, I'm afraid."

Lucky's heart sank. "You mean I have to stay here all night?" he asked.

"No need for that," the Colonel said kindly. "This calls for the Midnight Bark!"

The Colonel lumbered over to the door and howled into the night. Lucky waited anxiously for a response. At last, it came!

Bark! Bark! Bark!
Yip! Yip-yip! Yip, yip, yip!
Arf, arf, arooooo!

The barks echoed across the countryside to the Dalmatian Plantation, where a sleepy Pongo opened his eyes.

"It's a lost pup," he whispered to Perdita. "I'll go help."

"Follow the barks. They'll lead you home again," the Colonel told Lucky. "Good luck, lad!"

"Thank you," Lucky told the Colonel and Sergeant Tibs. Then, listening closely, he ran into the night. The Colonel was right. Following the sound of the barks, Lucky soon realised that he was on the path home. And now that he was less scared, Lucky was able to solve all the mysteries that he'd stumbled upon – even the creaky old gate that had started it all.

Back at the Dalmatian Plantation, Pongo was shocked to see Lucky bound up to him. "The Midnight Bark was for you?" he asked.

"Dad! Dad! I solved a mystery!" Lucky exclaimed. "Just like a real detective!"

"Tell me all about it in the morning," Pongo whispered as he led Lucky back to bed. "And no more mysteries tonight!"

Lucky agreed and snuggled up next to his siblings, ready to fall asleep after his big adventure. Suddenly, his ears twitched.

Cro-a-a-a-a-k-squeak!

What was that strange sound?

Maybe it was a clue!

![Disney] DUMBO

Dumbo's Snowy Day

Dumbo was a very special elephant – with his huge ears, he could soar through the sky like a bird. Dumbo performed in a circus with his mother, Mrs Jumbo. One chilly day, the circus animals were on their way to a new town. But their train, Casey Jr., was struggling to get through the falling snow. His wheels slid on the icy railroad tracks.

Finally, Casey Jr. decided it was too dangerous to keep going. The train came to a stop, and everyone waited for the snow to pass.

Dumbo was happy that the train had stopped. He'd never played in the snow before! He thought it felt awfully strange as he tried to walk through it. The snow pressed against his feet like cold sand.

"You can do it!" said Mrs Jumbo. She gave him a gentle nuzzle.

Soon Dumbo got the hang of walking through the snow. He liked the *crunch-crunch-crunch* sound he heard with every step.

All morning, Dumbo and his mother played in the snow.

They gathered snowballs together with their trunks. They made snow elephants. They even played hide-and-seek! But as Dumbo and his mother explored, they got farther and farther away from the waiting train.

Suddenly, Dumbo slid down a steep hill. He called for his mother to follow him. But when she reached the bottom of the hill, Mrs Jumbo realised she couldn't climb back up!

Dumbo tried to push. He tried to pull. But nothing worked. Mrs Jumbo slipped farther down the slope towards a sharp cliff's edge.

"You will have to fly off and get help," Mrs Jumbo told him.

So off Dumbo flew, as fast as his ears would take him. As he soared towards the train, the wind began to blow. It pushed harder and harder against him.

The snow stung his eyes, and the cold nipped at his toes.

Finally, Dumbo's ears got so cold he couldn't fly. As he waited for the wind to pass, he worried about his mother.

Once the wind died down, Dumbo raced back to the train. Quickly, he gathered all the animals together so that they could help.

"What are we waiting for?" Timothy Q. Mouse cried. "We've got to save Mrs Jumbo!"

Dumbo led his friends back to the cliff.

By the time they found Mrs Jumbo, the windstorm had pushed her even closer to the cliff's edge.

The animals knew they had to think of something – fast!

"Oh, dear," worried the giraffe. "How can we get down there to help?"

Timothy snapped his fingers – he had an idea. "Everybody line up!" he shouted. He ordered the animals to grab one another's tails.

At the front of the line, the ostrich leaned over the cliff to take hold of Mrs Jumbo's trunk.

"One, two, three, PULL!" Timothy yelled.

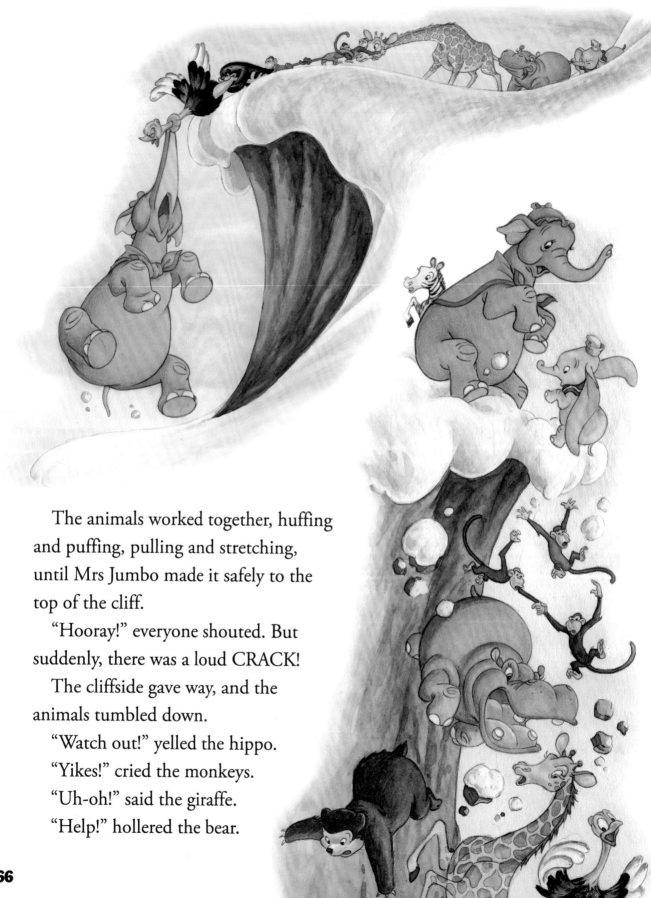

The animals worked together, huffing
and puffing, pulling and stretching,
until Mrs Jumbo made it safely to the
top of the cliff.

"Hooray!" everyone shouted. But
suddenly, there was a loud CRACK!

The cliffside gave way, and the
animals tumbled down.

"Watch out!" yelled the hippo.

"Yikes!" cried the monkeys.

"Uh-oh!" said the giraffe.

"Help!" hollered the bear.

All of the animals tumbled together and rolled down the hill.
Before long, they had become a giant snowball!

"How do you stop this thing?" Timothy shouted as they zoomed along.

The snowball gathered speed until...

Crash! Bang! Boom! Oof! The animal snowball hit the bottom of the hill and broke apart!

"Is everyone okay?" Timothy asked as he straightened his hat.

Luckily, everyone was fine – just a little dizzy from their unexpected snow ride. All the animals began walking back to the train. Walking wasn't nearly as fast as riding a snowball, but it was a lot less scary!

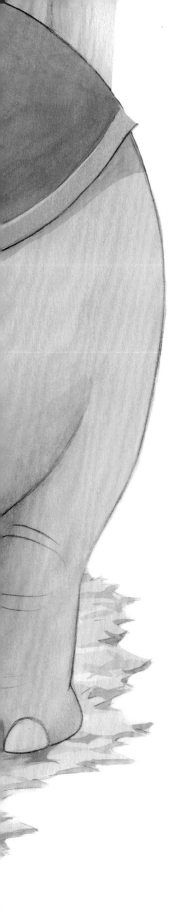

That night, Mrs Jumbo gave Dumbo a warm bath.

"Thank you for flying to find help today," Mrs Jumbo said to her son. "I'm so proud of you."

Dumbo smiled and blew a trunk full of water over his head.

"Hey! Don't forget about me," said Timothy from his teacup bath. "I helped, too!"

Mrs Jumbo nodded. "You certainly did. Thank you."

"Aw, gee," said Timothy. "It was nothing. Nothing at all."

Then it was time for bed. Dumbo snuggled up against his mother, and Timothy nestled underneath Dumbo's ear.

"Goodnight, my darling," Mrs Jumbo said softly.

"Sleep tight!" said Timothy.

Dumbo fell asleep right away. Tomorrow he and the circus animals would perform for hundreds of happy children in a new town. But for now, Dumbo was glad to be warm and safe with his mother as the snow fell gently outside.

Disney
ALICE
in
WONDERLAND

A Snack for the Queen

It was a lovely day in Wonderland. Alice was sitting in a garden, watching the bread-and-butterflies flitter from flower to flower.

"Why, their wings look just like buttered bread!" she exclaimed. "Everything here in Wonderland is so very curious."

As Alice looked around, she heard a voice behind her.

"Oh dear, oh dear, oh dear!"

Alice turned to see the White Rabbit running through the garden.
"Is everything all right?" she asked.

The White Rabbit stopped. "The Queen of Hearts is hungry, but
nothing in the palace seems to satisfy her. If I don't find her a
tasty treat soon, she'll have my head!"

"Perhaps I can help," Alice said. "I've never had any trouble finding something to eat in Wonderland. If we work together, I'm sure we will find something that makes the Queen happy."

The White Rabbit sighed. "I do hope you are right!" he said.

"Have you tried asking the Mad Hatter?" Alice asked. "His tea table is always filled with treats."

"Oh, no. I try to steer clear of the Hatter," the White Rabbit replied. "He's always causing trouble."

"That's true," Alice said. "But it's still worth a try."

Alice started down the path to the Mad Hatter's house. Suddenly, she stopped short.

"Perhaps we don't have to visit the Mad Hatter after all," she said, studying a bush. "Look at these cupcakes! Don't they look tasty?"

Alice plucked a cupcake from the bush, and she and the White Rabbit hurried to the palace.

"There you are!" the Queen of Hearts yelled when she spied the rabbit. Then she saw Alice. "You!" she shouted. "Off with your —"

Alice didn't give the Queen a chance to finish.

"We brought you a cupcake, Your Majesty," she said, handing the Queen the treat.

The Queen actually smiled. "Why, thank you," she said, reaching for it.

Before the Queen could take a bite, the cupcake began to move. Two wings opened up, and it flew away. It wasn't a cupcake at all. It was a bird!

Alice's eyes grew wide. The Queen would surely have her head now!

Alice and the White Rabbit quickly ran from the palace. They hadn't gone far when the Cheshire Cat appeared on the path in front of them.

"What's the hurry?" he asked them.

"We need to find a snack for the Queen," Alice replied.

The Cheshire Cat looked down at the berries on the bush beneath him. "Take her some of these blue berries," he suggested.

"But these aren't blueberries," Alice said. "They're red!"

"Red or blue, they're quite tasty," the Cheshire Cat said.

"The Queen is very impatient," the White Rabbit said. "And we don't have anything else to bring her..."

Alice agreed. It seemed they had no choice. She and the White Rabbit picked the berries and brought them to the Queen. She promptly gobbled them down.

"Delicious!" she cried. "I suppose you may keep your heads after all!"

But then the Queen noticed something: her fingers were blue!
So were her hands, and her arms...

"What have you done?" she shrieked.

"Oh, dear," Alice said. "That must be why the Cheshire Cat called them blue berries. They look red, but they turn you blue when you eat them!"

"Fix me!" the Queen yelled.

The White Rabbit nervously tapped his paws together. "Whatever will we do?"

"I have an idea," Alice said. She ran back to the bush where they had seen the Cheshire Cat. Next to it was a bush with blue berries.

She quickly picked some and hurried back to the Queen. "Eat these!" Alice urged her.

The Queen scowled. "Why should I trust you?"

"Well, I'm just guessing," Alice replied, "but if you don't try, you'll stay blue."

The Queen frowned and ate some of the blue berries. Slowly, the blue faded from her skin.

"I suppose that worked," the Queen said. "But I'm still hungry!"

Alice and the White Rabbit hurried off to find another snack for the Queen. Soon they bumped into Tweedledum and Tweedledee.

The twins were dancing and singing a silly song:

"When it comes to treats, we are not picky
We love a treat that's sweet and sticky
A snack you can eat when you need something quickie
It's lollipops for us!"

Alice noticed that each one was clutching two handfuls of yummy looking lollipops.

"Excuse me," she said. "We just happen to be looking for a tasty treat for the Queen. May we have a lollipop?"

"If it's for the Queen, we can't say no," said Tweedledum.

"So take a lollipop and go!" finished Tweedledee, handing Alice a bright red lollipop.

Alice and the White Rabbit quickly brought the red lollipop to the
Queen of Hearts.

"Hmmm," said the Queen. "I do like lollipops. And it is the perfect colour.
Let me give it a try."

She licked the lollipop and smiled. Then her face turned bright red
with heat.

"Spicy! Spicy!" she yelled. "Somebody bring me some water!"

While the guards rushed to help the Queen, Alice and the White Rabbit
slipped away from the palace again.

"That's it. I'm going to the Mad Hatter's house," Alice said. "I'm sure he
will have a good snack for the Queen."

"I'll wait here," the White Rabbit said.

Alice quickly made her way to the
Mad Hatter's house. She found him
serving tea to the March Hare.

"Excuse me," she said, "but I was wondering if you could help.
The White Rabbit and I need to bring the Queen of Hearts
a snack in a hurry. She's very hungry."

The March Hare's ears perked up. "The Queen, you said?"
He looked at the Mad Hatter.

"Yes, I did," Alice replied.

The Mad Hatter grinned. He handed a cookie to Alice.

"This is exactly what she needs," he promised.

So Alice and the White Rabbit brought the cookie to the Queen of Hearts. She sniffed it.

"It smells good," she said, frowning suspiciously. "And it looks tasty."

The Queen bit into the cookie. "It is tasty!" she exclaimed.

Suddenly, something very strange happened. The Queen began to shrink! She got smaller and smaller until she was no bigger than the cookie.

"Guards! Guards! Off with their heads!" she yelled. But her voice was so tiny and squeaky that the guards didn't hear her.

Alice and the White Rabbit hurried away.

"The Mad Hatter was right," Alice said with a giggle. "That cookie is exactly what the Queen needed!"